This Little Tiger book
belongs to:

_____

_____

_____

For Rich and my
Moon, TBFIL x – BD

For Evie May – DB

LITTLE TIGER PRESS LTD,
an imprint of the Little Tiger Group
1 Coda Studies, 189 Munster Road, London SW6 6AW
Imported into the EEA by Penguin Random House Ireland,
Morrison Chambers, 32 Nassau Street, Dublin D02 YH68
www.littletiger.co.uk

First published in Great Britain 2022 · This edition published 2022
Text by Becky Davies · Illustrations by Dana Brown
Text and illustrations copyright © Little Tiger Press Ltd 2021
A CIP catalogue record for this book is available from the
British Library · All rights reserved · ISBN 978-1-80104-028-0
Printed in China · LTP/2800/4546/0522
10 9 8 7 6 5 4 3 2 1

I Love You More than All the Stars

Becky Davies
Dana Brown

LITTLE TIGER
LONDON

I love you more
than all the

STARS

that shimmer
in the night.

Just as their glow lights up the sky,
my love shines STRONG and

BRIGHT.

ove you more than

SUMMER

DAYS

and more than

SUNSETS, TOO.

I love you deeper than the sea, its waves of ENDLESS BLUE.

I love you   STRONGER.

And
softer
than a
snowflake
dance

as crystals gently twirl.

HIGHER than the CLOUDS...

...and sweeter than the

BRAZIL NUT

I love you further than the

MOON

and then back home again.

I love you
LONGER
than a
day . . .

...a week, a month, a year.
My love lasts for eternity.

I love you wider
than the

WORLD

that shimmers
down below.

You're my best friend.

I LOVE YOU

more than you

will ever know.

More beautiful stories to fall in love with . . .

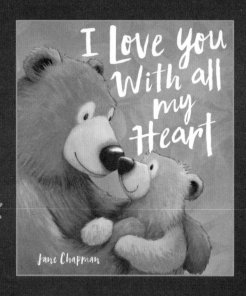

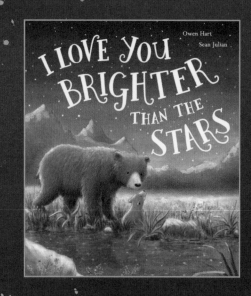

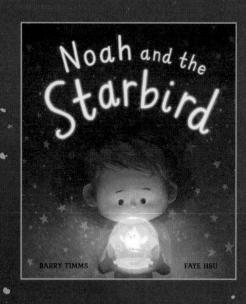

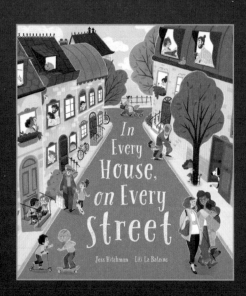

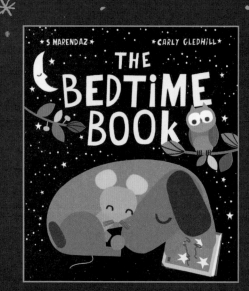

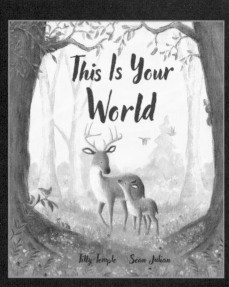